Island Birthday

Eva Murray

Illustrated by
Jamie Hogan

Tilbury House Publishers
Thomaston, Maine

"Mom! We're out of milk

. . . again!"

I am tired of this. The stormy weather has kept the mail plane away and the island fishermen's boats tied up in the harbor for days. My birthday is coming up. Grammy says she sent a package, but it won't come until the weather clears. I'm stuck here—eating cereal without milk and wondering about my birthday.

I tell Mom, "If we lived on the mainland then I'd get to have a normal birthday, with a bunch of kids my age and presents from a toy store."

Mom says, "Well, Grammy sent out some new party stuff. Why don't you go and visit Harv? Maybe he's got some milk."

Mom is always way too calm about these things.

"Harv, do you ever get sick of living on this island?"

"Sure, I get frustrated. I'm out of turpentine and red paint. I've been waiting for my art supplies for a week."

"Well, I think people have to be crazy to live on an island."

Harv says, "A lot of people think there's something really special about living way out to sea."

Then he asks, "Can you help me collect some driftwood? I have a lot of orders for my benches."

The beach is one of our favorite spots.
In the summer we spend whole days down there
—and some nights!

There are never any crowds.

One night last summer a few of us went swimming in the dark when there was phosphorescence in the water.

It looked like the ocean was on fire
and we were right in the middle of it.

But today the beach is windy and damp. Harv picks up a piece of blue sea glass and holds it up to look through it. "Sort of looks like the state of Maine, if you hold it right, don't you think?"

We find lots of driftwood for Harv's benches.

A loud bark makes us look up. Brewster runs over with his owner, Pat. "Not very nice today, is it?" Pat says. "I hope this weather clears and they fly soon. We're almost out of dog food."

"Hey Riley," she says. "Look what I found." She takes a perfect moon shell out of her pocket. "Haven't you got a birthday coming up?"

I never see moon shells unbroken. This one looks amazing.

We put Harv's driftwood in the truck and head over to the post office. Everybody is there as usual. Brian works on the newspaper crossword puzzle. Annie is telling Erica how to make apple butter.

From behind the counter, Ruth says, "I sure hope they fly soon! People keep calling me to find out if the mail has come yet. I ask them, 'Have you looked at the weather? Have you heard a plane? There is no mail yet!'" She shakes her head. I know how she feels.

Then she calls my name.

"Riley, I know you like planes. Come here and check out these stamps. They just came last week. It's a biplane called a Curtiss JN4—they called it a 'Jenny'—flying upside-down!"

I look more closely at the stamp.

"There's a good story behind this. A long time ago, the post office accidentally printed some airmail stamps with upside-down airplanes. Stamp collectors saved them, and now the old ones are worth a lot of money! This year they printed some more, but this time on purpose. Aren't they cool?"

All I can think of to say is, "I wish our mail plane would come, right-side-up or upside-down!"

I smile at Ruth and head outside.

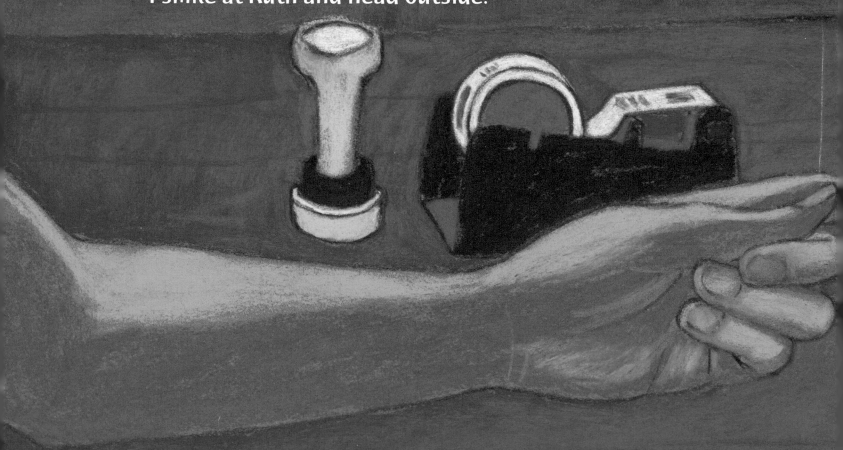

Ralph is working up on the phone lines.

"What's this?" I shout up at him.

"That's telephone wire. It's what's inside that heavy black cable up there. When my kids were little I used to bring home short pieces. They liked to make things out of it, little models and bendable wire people and rings and bracelets and stuff."

I think that sounds like fun.

"Let's hope the weather clears soon. The new wire cutters I ordered last week sure would come in handy."

Harv catches up to me. We stop to say hi to Captain Lauren. Her sternman is busy putting new rope on lobster traps. He jokes, "Hey, you want a job next summer? You can go 'third man' and bag the bait!"

I know what he's talking about. Lobster bait is slimy, stinky, rotten fish, but a lot of the big kids do that work on the boats. It pays much better than mowing lawns.

Lauren rolls her eyes. "You wouldn't like going to haul traps in this weather! The water's been looking angry all week. There's plenty of shop work to do, though. I've got six coils of rope coming on the airplane. Well, if we ever get an airplane! It sure has been a while! I guess it's . . ."

She trails off and cocks her head to listen.
We all listen hard.

There's a new sound in the air! It is still faint and far away. I look at the sky. The fog is lifting. The wind is still blowing some, but not as hard as yesterday. I listen hopefully.

All over the island, people hear the plane and head to the landing strip.

In the post office, Ruth says,

"Okay, everybody, I've got work to do!"

When the little Cessna 206 flies in
over the bay and rolls to a stop on
the gravel runway,
             everyone cheers!

"Looks like somebody's having a birthday!" says Ed the pilot with a smile. Then he gives a box to Harv.

"It's totally worth the wait," I tell Uncle Harv.
"Now we can celebrate—island style."

Tilbury House Publishers
12 Starr Street
Thomaston, Maine 04861
800-582-1899 • www.tilburyhouse.com

To Eli —EM
To Nikolai, and all island kids who make their own fun —JH

Library of Congress Cataloging-in-Publication Data

Murray, Eva, 1964- author.
 Island birthday / by Eva Murray ; illustrated by Jamie Hogan.
   pages cm
 Summary: As Riley anxiously awaits the plane that will bring a birthday
present from his grandmother, he goes visiting in his island community and
discovers that others are at least as eager for the storm to clear so that they
can get items they need or want.
  ISBN 978-0-88448-425-7 (hardcover) -- ISBN 978-0-88448-426-4 (ebook)
 [1. Community life--Fiction. 2. Islands--Fiction. 3. Storms--Fiction. 4. Postal
service--Fiction. 5. Birthdays--Fiction.] I. Hogan, Jamie, illustrator. II. Title.
 PZ7.M875Isl 2015
 [Fic]--dc23

2014042482

Designed by Kathy Squires

Printed by Shenzhen Caimei Printing Co., Ltd., February 2015
(43537-0/121714.2)